All children have a great ambition to read to themselves... and a sense of achievement when they can do so.

The **read it yourself** *series has been devised to satisfy their ambition. Even before children begin to learn to read formally, perhaps using a reading scheme, it is important that they have books and stories which will actively encourage the development of essential pre-reading skills. Books at Level 1 in this series have been devised with this in mind and will supplement pre-reading books available in any reading scheme.*

Children need to develop left to right eye movements and to perceive differences in word and letter shapes. Based on well-known nursery rhymes and games which children will have heard, these simple pre-readers introduce key words and phrases which children will meet in later reading. These are repeated and the full-colour artwork provides picture clues for new words.

Many young children will remember the words rather than read them but this is a normal part of pre-reading. It is recommended that the parent or teacher should read the book aloud to the child first and then go through the story, with the child reading the text.

British Library Cataloguing in Publication Data
Murdock, Hy
   Here we go round the mulberry bush. —
   (Read it yourself. Level 1; no. 2)
   1. Readers—1950-
   I. Title   II. Russell, Chris · III. Series
   428.6   PE1119
   ISBN 0-7214-0891-5

First edition

© LADYBIRD BOOKS LTD MCMLXXXV

Here we go round the Mulberry Bush

devised by Hy Murdock
illustrated by Chris Russell
of Hurlston Design Ltd

Ladybird Books Loughborough

Here we go round
the mulberry bush
on a cold and frosty
morning.

This is the way
I clean my teeth.

I wash my face.

We brush our hair.

The girl drinks her milk.

The boy eats his egg.

The girl and boy
clean their
shoes.

We can play
on a cold and frosty
morning.

This is the way
I can run.

I can jump.

We can swing.

The girl can ride her bike.

The boy can play
on his skates.

The girl and boy can play with a ball.

We can help on a cold
and frosty morning.

I can wash
the clothes.

I can brush
the dog.

We can clean
the car.

The girl and boy
feed the birds.

Here we go round the mulberry bush

on a cold and frosty
morning.